HERE COMES THE POO BUS!

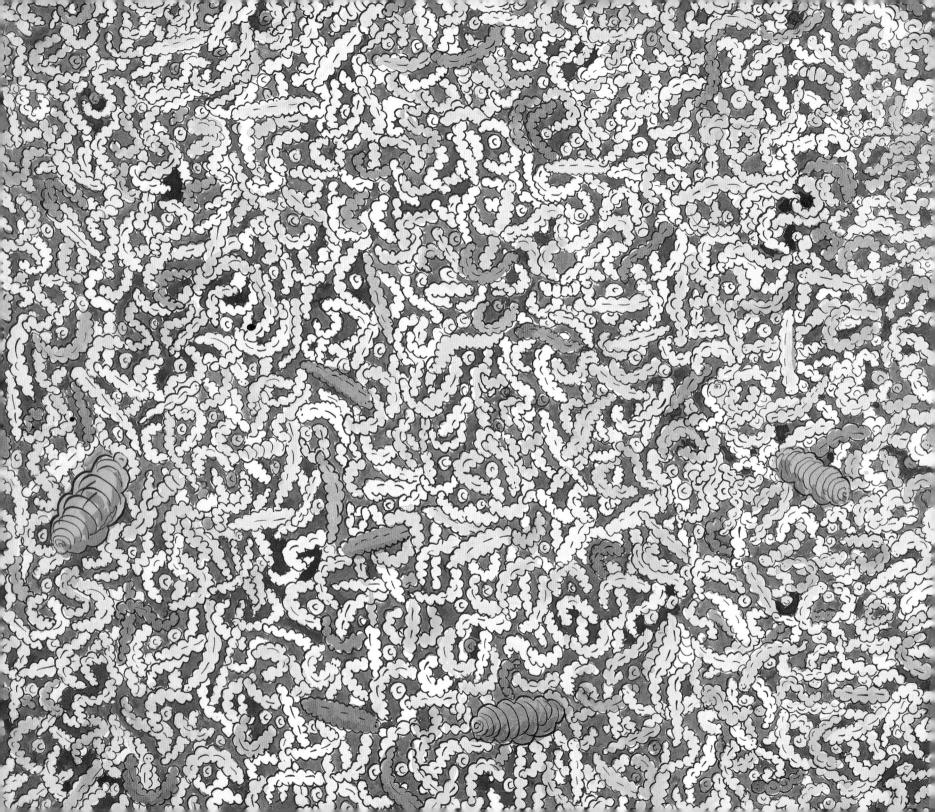

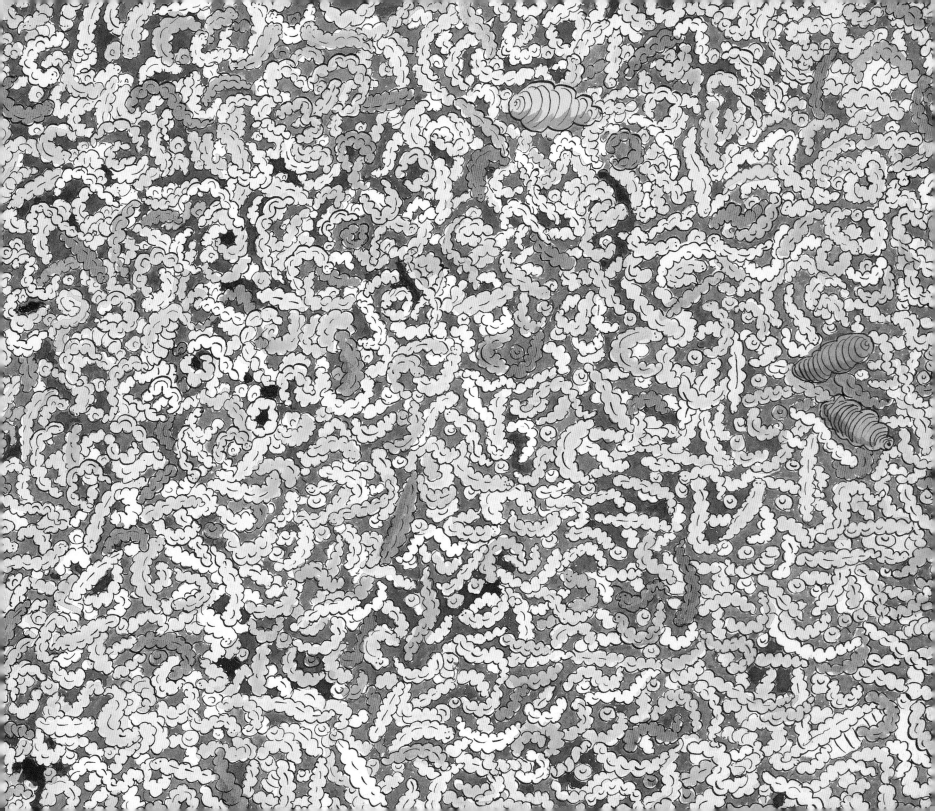

FOR GENE AND DEAN WEEN — A.S.

FOR MUM AND DAD — N.D-B.

Published by the Penguin Group: London, New York,
Australia, Canada, India, Ireland, New Zealand and South Africa
Penguin Books Ltd, Registered Offices:
80 Strand, London WC2R 0RL, England
puffinbooks.com
This edition published 2012
001 – 10 9 8 7 6 5 4 3 2 1
Text copyright © Andy Stanton, 2011
Illustrations copyright © Noëlle Davies-Brock, 2011
The moral right of the author and illustrator has been asserted
Made and printed in China
ISBN: 978–0–141–33400–4

HERE COMES THE POO BUS!

ANDY STANTON

PUFFIN

Illustrated by
NOËLLE DAVIES-BROCK

Here it comes! The poo bus!
Rolling down the road
Picking up the insects
Driven by **Uncle Toad.**

"All aboard the poo bus! All aboard!" he cries
"We're going to the seaside for a lovely big surprise!"

Here's the conductor, Beetle Bill
His job? To ring the bells
"I love this bus," says Beetle Bill,
"I love the way it smells."

Here it comes! The poo bus!
Steaming down the street
Picking up the insects
For a lovely seaside treat!

"Hop aboard the poo bus!
Hop on!" cries Uncle Toad
"The seaside's fun so won't you let me
Drive you down the road?"

First is **Mrs Housefly**
With her children, one, two, three

The poo bus picks them up and then
It's off to the sea!

Here it comes! The poo bus!
Along the avenue
It's big! It's brown! It drives through town!
It's made out of poo!

"Climb aboard the poo bus!
Climb on!" cries Uncle T.

"No time to waste! Get in, my friends!
We're going to the sea!"

Next on is Daddy Long-Legs
Who needs two seats, not one
"You must pay double," says Beetle Bill
"I'm sorry, my lanky chum."

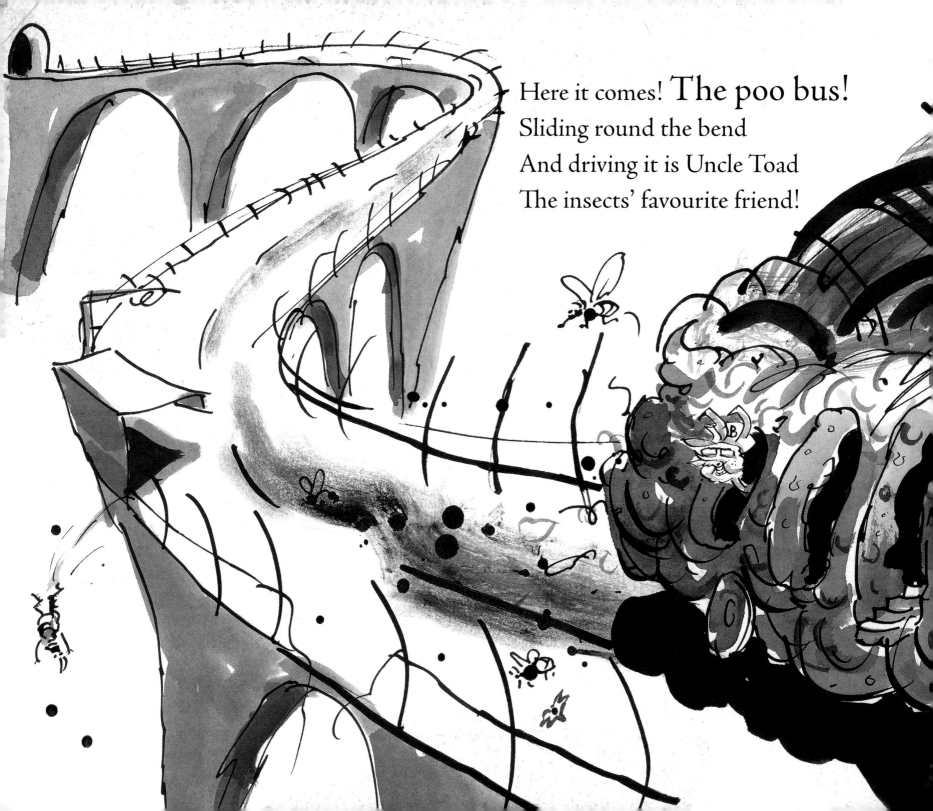

Here it comes! The poo bus!
Sliding round the bend
And driving it is Uncle Toad
The insects' favourite friend!

"Jump on!" cries Uncle Toad now
"Jump on, I say, jump on!
We'll make it to the sandy beach
Before the sunshine's gone!"

"Take me to the seaside, please,"
Says **Madame Claire** the Spider
"And take us too, oh, take us, do!"
Beg twenty flies inside her.

Inside Madame Claire the Spider...

BOING!

Here it comes! The poo bus!
Flying down the hill
With Mrs Housefly, Daddy Long-Legs,
Claire and Beetle Bill.
And . . .

"Join us on the poo bus!
Join us!" cries Uncle Toad
"There's room for more, so join us please!
Oh, what a heavy load!"

"Oh, no," says Mrs Housefly,
"It's **nasty Fred,** who stings."

But clever Madame Claire the Spider
Traps his naughty wings.

Here it comes! **The poo bus!** Whizzing through the sands
"We're nearly there!" shouts Daddy Long-Legs, clapping all his hands.

"Hop off! Hop off!" cries Uncle Toad. "Our journey's at an end . . .

Gobble! Gobble! Down they go!
He eats them, every one
And Bill gets all the little scraps
Once Uncle Toad is done.

The poo bus turns, the sign is changed
The sun is going down.
"Hop on! Hop on!" cries Uncle Toad,
"We're going to the town!"

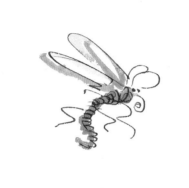